JOURNEY T

Beverley Naidoo was born i̶n̶... and came to England when she was twenty-one. She married another South African exile and was only able to return freely to her country twenty-six years later, after Nelson Mandela's release from jail. Her two children were brought up in England.

The award-winning *Journey to Jo'burg* was her first book. It opened a window onto apartheid for many children worldwide, but was banned in South Africa until 1991. Her fiction includes a sequel, *Chain of Fire*, and *No Turning Back*, which was shortlisted for the Guardian Award. She has written picture books, including the *Letang and Julie* series, short stories and poetry.

For many years she taught children with reading difficulties and she has been an Adviser for English and Cultural Diversity. Her work for teachers includes *Through Whose Eyes?*, a doctoral study of teenage responses to literature and racism. She is a Visiting Fellow at the University of Southampton School of Education and continues to work with children and adults in Britain and abroad as a writer, storyteller and education adviser.

Collins Modern Classics

Journey to Jo'burg

A South African Story

by

Beverley Naidoo

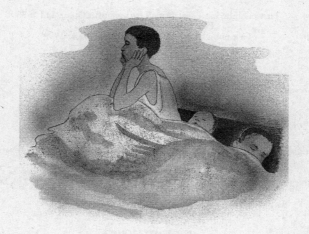

Illustrated by Lisa Kopper

Collins
An imprint of HarperCollins*Publishers*

First published in Great Britain by Longman Group Ltd 1985
First published by Collins 1987
First published as a Collins Modern Classic 1999

1 3 5 7 9 10 8 6 4 2

Collins Modern Classics is an imprint of
HarperCollins*Publishers* Ltd, 77–85 Fulham Palace Road,
Hammersmith, London W6 8JB.

The HarperCollins website address is
www.**fire**and**water**.com

ISBN 0 00 675455-4

Printed and bound in Great Britain by
Caledonian International Book Manufacturing Ltd, Glasgow, G64

In memory of two small children
who died far away from their mother…
and to Mary, their Mma, who worked in Jo'burg.

The idea for this book arose at meetings of the Education Group of the British Defence and Aid Fund for Southern Africa in 1985. BDAFSA was established by the late Canon Collins of St Paul's Cathedral in 1958 with the following objectives:

- to aid, defend and rehabilitate victims of unjust legislation, oppressive and arbitrary procedures
- to support their families and dependants
- to keep the conscience of the world alive to the issues at stake in Southern Africa
- to assist in the development of a non-racial society based on a democratic way of life.

With the election of South Africa's first democratic government, BDAFSA's work came to an end in 1994. However, its commitment to education for a non-racial society carries on through the Canon Collins Educational Trust for Southern Africa, which continues to benefit from sales of this work.

Can you imagine having to live apart from your parents for most of your childhood?

In South Africa for a long time the law forced many parents and children apart. Many fathers and mothers from the countryside had to go away to towns and cities to work. Their children had to stay behind. For this was the land of apartheid – where the broken families were all black and the people who made the laws were white. We didn't often hear about the children who were cut off from their parents. We only got a glimpse of them through a short news item now and then.

Joyous end to hunt for mum

It was a joyous reunion yesterday for the schoolgirl who came to the big city in search of her mother – only with the little knowledge that she worked in Vincent...

It began as a door-to-door search in the hope that one of the knocks would be answered by her mother...

(*The Daily Dispatch*, 1/10/81)

Another report told of a boy who had always lived with his mother until he was caught up in a police raid and taken hundreds of miles away.

Boy of 11 attempted 1, 289 km walk

An eleven-year-old boy who tried walking from Umtata in Transkei to Cape Town to be with his mother was reunited with her yesterday...

The boy said he had been born in Cape Town. Umtata was a strange place to him.

Asked why he wanted to walk back, he said simply: "My mother was in Cape Town and I wanted to be with her."

(*The Cape Times*, 26/9/81)

In April 1994, for the first time ever, South Africans of all backgrounds were able to vote for a new parliament. Nelson Mandela became the new President. He had been locked in jail for twenty-seven years because he had fought against apartheid *and racism. He wanted a country where black and white would be equal.*

It will take a long time to repair the damage of apartheid. Journey to Jo'burg *may help you understand why. But many people have planted their hopes, like seeds. Now they need to work hard at helping them grow.*

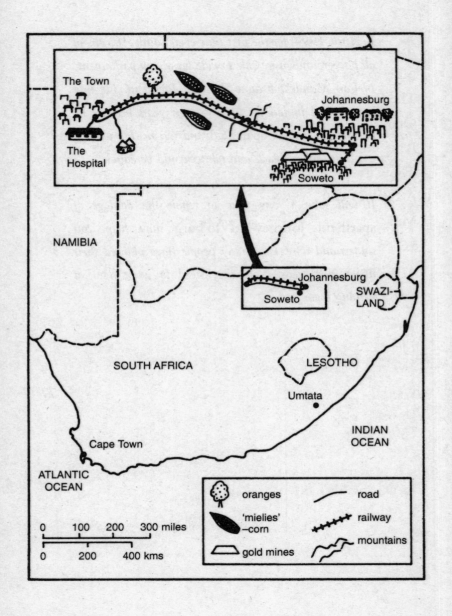

The Town

The Hospital

Johannesburg

Soweto

NAMIBIA

Johannesburg

Soweto

SWAZI-LAND

SOUTH AFRICA

LESOTHO

Umtata

INDIAN OCEAN

Cape Town

ATLANTIC OCEAN

0   100   200   300 miles

0   200   400 kms

oranges

'mielies' –corn

gold mines

road

railway

mountains

CONTENTS

Chapter One

NALEDI'S PLAN

NALEDI AND TIRO were worried. Their baby sister Dineo was ill, very ill. For three days now, Nono their granny had been trying to cool her fever with damp cloths placed on her little head and body. Mmangwane[1], their aunty, made her take sips of water, but still their sister lay hot and restless, crying softly at times.

"Can't we take Dineo to the hospital?" Naledi begged, but Nono said Dineo was much too sick to be carried that far. The only hospital was many miles away, and Naledi also knew they had no money to pay a doctor to visit them. No one in the village had that much money.

[1] "little mother" in Tswana.

"If only Mma[1] was here," Naledi wished over and over as she and Tiro walked down to the village tap with their empty buckets. She clutched tightly at the coins in her hand.

Each morning the children had to pass the place of graves on their way to buy the day's water and only last week another baby in the village had died. It was always scary seeing the little graves, but especially this fresh one now.

As they came nearer, Naledi fixed her eyes on the ground ahead, trying not to look, trying not to think. But it was no use. She just couldn't stop herself thinking of her own little sister being lowered into a hole in the ground.

Finally Naledi could stand it no longer. When they had returned with the water, she called Tiro to the back of the house and spoke bluntly.

"We must get Mma, or Dineo is going to die!"

"But how?" Tiro was bewildered.

Their mother worked and lived in Johannesburg, more than 300 kilometres away.

"We can get to the big road and walk," Naledi replied calmly.

It was the school holidays now, but in term-time it

---

[1] "mother" in Tswana.

took the children more than an hour to walk to school each day, so they were used to walking. Naledi wasn't going to let herself think how much longer it would take to get to Johannesburg.

However, Tiro was not so sure.

"But Nono doesn't want us to worry Mma and I know she won't let us go!"

"That's just it." Naledi retorted quickly. "Nono and Mmangwane keep saying Dineo will be better soon. You heard them talking last night. They say they don't want to send Mma a telegram and frighten her. But what if they wait and it's too late?"

Tiro thought for a moment.

"Can't we send Mma a telegram?"

"How can we if we haven't the money? And if we borrow some, Nono will hear about it and be very cross with us."

It was clear that Naledi had made up her mind – and Tiro knew his sister. She was four years older than him, already thirteen, and once she had decided something, that was that.

So Tiro gave up reasoning.

The children went to find Naledi's friend Poleng, and

explained. Poleng was very surprised but agreed to help. She would tell Nono once the children had gone and she also promised to help their granny, bringing the water and doing the other jobs.

"How will you eat on the way?" Poleng asked.

Tiro looked worried, but Naledi was confident.

"Oh, we'll find something."

Poleng told them to wait and ran into her house, returning soon with a couple of sweet potatoes and a bottle of water. The children thanked her. She was indeed a good friend.

Before they could go, Naledi had to get the last letter Mma had sent, so they would know where to look for her in the big city. Slipping into the house, Naledi took the letter quietly from the tin without Nono or Mmangwane noticing. Both were busy with Dineo as Naledi slipped out again.

Chapter Two

THE ROAD

THE CHILDREN WALKED quickly away from the village. The road was really just a track made by car tyres. Two lines of dusty red earth leading out across the flat dry grassland.

Once at the big tar road, they turned in the direction of the early morning sun, for that was the way to Johannesburg. The steel railway line glinted alongside the road.

"If only we had some money to buy tickets for the train. We don't have even one cent." Tiro sighed.

"Never mind. We'll get there somehow!" Naledi was still confident as they set off eastwards.

The tar road burnt their feet.

"Let's walk at the side," Tiro suggested.

The grass was dry and scratchy, but they were used to it. Now and again, a car or a truck roared by, and then the road was quiet again and they were alone. Naledi began to sing the words of her favourite tune and Tiro was soon joining in.

On they walked.

"Can't we stop and eat?" Tiro was beginning to feel sharp stabs of hunger. But Naledi wanted to go on until they reached the top of the long, low hill ahead.

Their legs slowed down as they began the walk uphill, their bodies feeling heavy. At last they came to the top and flopped down to rest.

Hungrily they ate their sweet potatoes and drank the water. The air was hot and still. Some birds skimmed lightly across the sky as they gazed down at the long road ahead. It stretched into the distance, between fenced-off fields and dry grass, up to another far-off hill.

"Come on! We must get on." Naledi insisted, pulling herself up quickly.

She could tell that Tiro was already tired, but they

couldn't afford to stop for long. The sun had already passed its midday position and they didn't seem to have travelled very far.

On they walked, steadily, singing to break the silence.

But in the middle of the afternoon, when the road led into a small town, they stopped singing and began to walk a little faster. They were afraid a policeman might stop them because they were strangers.

Policemen were dangerous. Even in their village they knew that...

The older children at school had made up a song:

> *"Beware that policeman,*
> *He'll want to see your 'pass'* [1]*,*
> *He'll say it's not in order,*
> *That day may be your last!"*

Grown-ups were always talking about this "pass". If you wanted to visit some place, the "pass" must allow it. If you wanted to change your job, the "pass" must allow it. It seemed everyone in school knew somebody who had been in trouble over the "pass".

Naledi and Tiro remembered all too clearly the terrible

---

[1] Every black South African over 16 years has to carry a "passbook" at all times. It names the place where that person has to live and work.

stories their uncle had told them about a prison farm. One day he had left his "pass" at home and a policeman had stopped him. That was how he got sent to the prison farm.

So, without even speaking, Naledi and Tiro knew the fear in the other's heart as they walked through the strange town. They longed to look in some of the shop windows, but they did not dare stop. Nervously they hurried along the main street, until they had left the last house of the town behind them.

Chapter Three

ORANGES!

ON THEY WALKED. The sun was low down now and there was a strong smell of oranges coming from rows and rows of orange trees behind barbed wire fences. As far as they could see there were orange trees with dark green leaves and bright round fruit. Oranges were sweet and wonderful to taste and they didn't have them often.

The children looked at each other.

"Do you think we could…" Tiro began.

But Naledi was already carefully pushing apart the barbed wire, edging her body through.

"Keep watch!" she ordered Tiro.

She was on tiptoes, stretching for an orange, when they heard, "HEY, YOU!"

Naledi dropped down, then dashed for the fence. Tiro was holding the wires for her. She tried to scramble through, but it was too late. A hand grasped her and pulled her back.

Naledi looked up and saw a young boy, her own age.

"What are you doing?" he demanded.

He spoke in Tswana, their own language.

"The white farmer could kill you if he sees you. Don't you know he has a gun to shoot thieves?"

"We're not thieves. We've been walking all day and we're very hungry. Please don't call him." Naledi pleaded.

The boy looked more friendly now and asked where they came from.

So they told him about Dineo and how they were going to Johannesburg. The boy whistled.

"Phew. So far!"

He paused.

"Look. I know a place where you can sleep tonight and where the farmer won't find you. Stay here and I'll take you there when it's dark."

Naledi and Tiro glanced at each other, still a little nervous.

"Don't worry. You'll be safe waiting here. The farmer has gone inside for his supper," the boy reassured them. Then he grinned. "But if you eat oranges you must hide the peels well or there will be big trouble. We have to pick the fruit, but we're not allowed to eat it."

He turned and ran off, calling softly, "See you later."

"Can we stay here for the night?" Tiro asked.

Naledi wasn't too sure if they should.

"It can go badly if the farmer finds us. Remember what happened to Poleng's brother?"

When Poleng's brother had been caught taking a mielie[1], the poor boy had been whipped until he couldn't stand up any more.

Tiro bit his lip.

"But we can leave early in the morning before the farmer is up, can't we?"

"Well… I expect we must sleep somewhere, or we'll be too tired to walk tomorrow," Naledi agreed slowly.

So Tiro slipped through the barbed wire and together they picked some oranges. It seemed a bit safer now that it was getting darker. Four large oranges were enough for Naledi, but Tiro kept on picking and eating more.

"You'll be sick if you stuff yourself like that," warned his sister.

Still he took no notice, until suddenly he clutched his tummy.

"Ooooh!" he groaned.

Naledi just said, "What did I tell you? Come on, we must hide the peels."

With two sharp stones they began to dig a hole. Tiro made odd little grunts from the pain in his tummy, but he dug well even though the ground was hard and dry. After burying the peel and filling up the hole, they

---

[1] a corn on the cob

searched around for stones and dry leaves to cover over the freshly dug soil.

They sat close together, shivering a little from the night chill. Naledi had begun to wonder if the boy really would return, when they heard the sound of soft running footsteps. The shape in the dark was that of the boy worker.

"Come!" he beckoned, and began to lead the way through rows and rows of orange trees.

They stumbled along, hardly able to see, but at last they came to a shed.

"You'll be warm with the sacks," the boy said quietly as he let them in. Then, shyly, he took out a tin plate from under a sack. "I brought you a little pap[1]. I'm sorry but that's all we get here most days."

"Thank you, thank you," Tiro and Naledi whispered.

"*Sala sentle*,"[2] said the boy as he slipped away in the dark.

"*Tsamaya sentle*,"[3] came the reply from the shed.

---

[1] porridge made from corn-meal
[2] "Stay well": farewell greeting in Tswana
[3] "Go well": farewell greeting in Tswana

Chapter Four

RIDE ON A LORRY

TIRO WOKE WHEN he heard the rooster crow. The shed was already half light. He shook Naledi.

"Get up! We must hurry!"

As they crept out from the shed, they saw the farm buildings a little distance away, with thin smoke rising from the chimney.

Silently they ran through the long grass towards the orange trees. Then through the orange trees, row after row, until there at last was the barbed wire.

Finding the road again, they almost felt happy! The road was cool from the night and they sang as they walked.

The sun rose higher. On they walked. The heat sank into

them and they felt the sweat on their bodies. On they walked. Alone again, except for the odd flashing by of a car or a truck.

SCREECH! Tyres skidded and stopped.

"Where are you two kids going?"

The driver of the lorry stuck a friendly face out of the window.

"To Johannesburg, Rra."[1]

"Are you crazy? That's more than 250 kilometres away!"

"We have to go," Naledi said simply, and explained.

"Well, well, that's something!" the driver muttered. "It will take you about a week to walk that far and your granny will be very worried. I should take you back home, but I'm late today already."

He paused to think. "Do you know where your mother works?"

Naledi nodded, pulling out the letter from her pocket.

"All right then. Hop on the back and I'll take you to Jo'burg. I'm taking the oranges there."

"Thank you, Rra!"

The children laughed. They pulled themselves up onto the lorry, wedging themselves against the sacks of oranges. So they were really on their way! And it was

---

[1] "father" in Tswana. The children are being polite to an older person.

their first time on a lorry too!

The engine started up and the lorry was soon thundering along. Walking had been so quiet but travelling in a lorry was very noisy. The air which had been so hot and still before, now swept past their faces. The land which had stood still, now seemed to rush by.

Thorn bushes, telegraph poles, wire fences, ploughed fields, cattle, rows of oranges, tall gum trees by a farm house… Almost as soon as they had seen something, it was gone.

Little by little, Tiro began to lean further out over the side to feel the wind on his face. Naledi called.

"Sit back or you'll fall!" but her brother took no notice.

Suddenly the lorry went over a bump and Tiro jerked forwards. Naledi grabbed him just in time.

"Didn't I tell you?" she shouted over the noise of the lorry.

A little shaken, Tiro mumbled, "Sorry", and settled back properly against the orange sacks. Together they watched the road stretching far out behind them.

As the lorry sped on its way through the countryside, the

children saw how the land was changing. Where they lived the land was almost flat, with few hills. Now for the first time, they were seeing proper mountains with steep rocks and crags. In some places it looked as if the road had been cut through the rock. Naledi was wondering how people could cut through rock, when Tiro asked her, "Where shall we find Mma in Jo'burg?"

His sister took the letter from her pocket and stared at the words at the top of the page.

"It's a place called 'Parktown'," she read slowly.

Tiro took the letter and studied the words too.

Naledi began to think of their mother and how, when Mma visited them, her first remarks were always about how they must work hard at school. When they had asked Mma why she worked so far away from home, her reply had been, "How else can I find the money to send you to school?"

But it was still very strange, thought Naledi.

Once she had asked Mma, "Why can't we live with you in the city? We could go to school there, couldn't we?"

Mma had seemed upset, but just said, "The white people who make the laws don't allow it. That's how it is."

But why not? Why not? thought Naledi.

Chapter Five

THE CITY OF GOLD

THE LORRY JOLTED to a stop and the driver came round to the back.

"OK?" he asked. "You can stretch your legs for a minute."

He helped them down.

"Your lorry is very fast," Tiro said.

"Yes! But it's not *my* lorry. I only drive it for the baas."[1]

They didn't stop for long because the driver had to get to Johannesburg and return the same day.

"Look out for the mine dumps," he told the children, as they climbed back up. "It's the earth they dig up to get to the gold. Jo'burg is the city of gold, so they say!" He gave a dry laugh.

[1] 'boss'

The children looked oddly at each other.

"What's the matter?" the driver asked.

The children were silent for a moment. Then Naledi said quietly, "Our father worked in a mine and he got sick with the coughing sickness. He died there."

"*Awu! Awu!* That's bad!" the driver shook his head.

The children watched out for the mine dumps. When their father was alive he used to come home once a year. He would tell them about the great dark holes and passages under the earth.

"But Rra, why do you go away for so long?" they remembered asking him.

"To get money so you can eat, my children."

Nor could they forget his last visit. The terrible coughing in the night and Nono's soft worried voice.

Now these mountains of sand had taken their father for ever. Naledi put her arms round Tiro.

The countryside disappeared and soon buildings seemed to follow buildings without end.

"This must be Jo'burg!" exclaimed Naledi, as the lorry raced along a great wide road towards tall shapes which speared up into the sky. There was noise, smoke and a horrid smell coming from the traffic. So many cars, so many people!

"How shall we find Mma?" Tiro whispered.

"We'll find her somehow," Naledi comforted.

The lorry began to slow down. The buildings now seemed to be crowding in on them. Naledi and Tiro sat tightly together, trying not to feel frightened.

Finally the lorry shuddered to a complete stop and the driver came round to the back.

"This is where I unload. I would like to take you safely to your mother, but my time here is too short. Wait here while I find the right bus for you."

"But we..." Tiro began, but the driver had already disappeared into the crowd. He was back soon.

"There's a bus stop just round the corner for Parktown. Come, I'll show you."

"But we don't have money for the bus, so we have to walk," Tiro now managed to tell the driver.

"What children! You've got a lot of guts, but you know nothing about Jo'burg. It's dangerous! You can't walk here on your own. Here, take this!"

He pushed a few coins into Naledi's hand and before the children had finished thanking him, he began to steer them through the crowd.

At the bus stop he explained how they must say where they were going and ask where to get off the bus.

"You don't need to wait with us here, Rra. We'll be all right now," Naledi assured the driver.

He didn't seem happy about leaving them on their own, but Naledi insisted they could manage. It would be too bad if he got into trouble. The children thanked him again and they made their farewells, before he was swallowed up once more amongst the city people.

Chapter Six

A New Friend

As they turned towards the road, there was a bus with the word 'PARKTOWN' in big letters on the front. It was slowing down a little way up the road and the doors were opening. Through the front windscreen they could see the driver was black.

"Come on, Tiro!" called Naledi, pulling him by the arm. They were just about to jump aboard, when someone shouted at them in English, "What's wrong with you? Are you stupid?"

Startled, they looked up at the angry face of the bus driver and then at the bus again. White faces stared at them from inside as the bus moved off.

Naledi and Tiro stood on the side of the road, shaken,

holding hands tightly, when a voice behind them said, "Don't let it bother you. That's what they're like. You'd better come out of the road."

A young woman put out her hand to bring them onto the pavement.

"You must be strangers here if you don't know about the buses. This stop has a white sign, but we have to wait by the black one over there."

She pointed to a small black metal signpost.

"You must also look at the front of the bus for the small notice saying 'Non-whites only'."

"I'm sorry. We forgot to look," Naledi explained.

"It's not you who should be sorry!" said the young woman forcefully. "They should be sorry, those stupid people! Why shouldn't we use any bus? When our buses are full, their buses are half empty. Don't you be sorry!"

The children glanced at each other. This person was different from their mother. Mma never spoke out like that.

Naledi took out the letter and when the young woman looked at the address, she exclaimed, "But this is near where my mother works. I'm on my way to visit her today, so I can show you the place."

"Thank you, Mma,"[1] the children smiled. Lucky again.

"By the way, I'm Grace Mbatha. Now, who are you both, and where are you from? You speak Tswana the way my mother does. Maybe you live near my mother's people."

So, once again, the children began their story.

Luckily the bus wasn't full when it arrived. Grace had warned them that in the rush hour you were almost squeezed to death. As the bus trundled along, stopping and starting with the traffic, there was a chance to stare out of the windows. Tiro thought the cyclists were very brave, riding in between all the cars. Naledi kept trying

---

[1] "mother" in Tswana. The children are being polite to an older person.

to see the tops of the tall buildings, twisting her neck round until it began to hurt.

The bus now heaved its way up a steep hill and soon they were leaving the city buildings, seeing the sky again, as well as trees, grass lawns and flowers either side of the road. Behind the trees were big houses, such as they had never seen before. Grace smiled at the way the children were staring as if amazed.

"Don't you know the people in this place have a lot of money? My mother looks after two children in a very big house and there is another person just to cook and another person to look after the garden."

Naledi and Tiro listened with interest. Mma never liked to talk much to them about her work when she was at home, although once they had overheard Mma talking to Nono about the child whom she looked after. Mma had said "The little girl is very rude. She thinks I belong to her mother. You should hear how she can shout at me."

Naledi wanted to ask Grace to tell them some more, but she was still a little shy, and soon they had reached their stop.

They stepped off the bus onto a wide pavement along a street lined with great leafy trees.

"That's the road where your mother works, at number 25. My Mma works at number 17 in the next road down there. Can you manage now?"

The children nodded, and then Grace added, "If you need somewhere to stay tonight, you can come back with me to Soweto. I'm going home at six o'clock, OK?"

Tiro and Naledi thanked Grace, although they were a little puzzled about needing somewhere to stay. After all, they would be with their mother now and they would be going home with her as quickly as possible, back to Dineo.

As they turned to go down the road, they suddenly felt very excited – and anxious too. So much had been happening that they hadn't been thinking all along of their little sister.

"Please let her be all right," now pounded in Naledi's brain.

Half-walking, half-running, they made for number 25.

Chapter Seven

MMA

THERE IT STOOD, a great pink house with its own grass lawn and trees in front, even its own road leading up to the front door! The two children stopped at the wide iron gates, looking up to it. The gates were closed, with a notice on them: BEWARE OF THE DOG.

"Are we allowed in?" Tiro whispered.

"We must go in," Naledi replied, opening the gate a little.

Nervously they slipped in and slowly walked up the drive to the large front door. Before they dared to knock, they heard a fierce barking from inside which made them grip each other's hands, ready to run back to the street. Then they heard a sharp voice inside call out, in English, "Joyce, see who it is!"

The door opened…

As Mma gasped, the children flung themselves at her and she clasped them in her arms, hugging them. Tears welled up in her eyes as the children sobbed against her.

"What is wrong? What is wrong?" Mma cried softly.

"Who is it, Joyce?" came a brisk voice from behind. The dog was still barking.

"Be quiet, Tiger!" ordered the brisk voice, and the barking stopped.

Mma stifled her sobs.

"Madam, these are my children."

"What are they doing here?" asked the white lady.

"Madam, I don't know. They haven't told me yet."

"Dineo is very ill, Mma," Naledi spoke between sobs. "Her fever won't go away. Nono and Mmangwane don't want to trouble you, but I told Tiro we must come and bring you home."

Mma gasped again and held her children more tightly.

"Madam, my little girl is very sick. Can I go home to see her?"

The Madam raised her eyebrows.

"Well, Joyce, I can't possibly let you go today. I need you tonight to stay in with Belinda. The Master and I are going to a very important dinner party…"

She paused.

"But I suppose you can go tomorrow."

"Thank you, Madam."

"I hope you realise how inconvenient this will be for me. If you are not back in a week, I shall just have to look for another maid, you understand?"

"Yes, Madam."

The children couldn't follow everything the Madam was saying in English, but her voice sounded annoyed, while Mma spoke so softly. Why does the white lady seem cross with Mma? It's not Mma's fault that Dineo is sick, Naledi thought.

The children huddled close to Mma's starched white apron. They hadn't seen her in this strange servant's uniform before.

As Mma led the children through to the kitchen, they glanced across at open doors leading into other large rooms. A wide staircase also led upwards. Never had they imagined a house could be this size!

In the kitchen Mma gave them a drink of water and some porridge she had cooked earlier. The kitchen seemed like a picture out of a magazine Mma had once brought home from the Madam. Their mother must have been busy cleaning that afternoon because glistening plates, of different sizes, cups and saucers and delicate glasses were neatly stacked close to a large empty cupboard.

Naledi noticed that Mma took the tin plates and mugs for them from a separate little cupboard. While they ate, Mma quickly got on with her work.

When she had finished, she took the children to her room at the back of the yard. The children looked around the little room with interest. On the big iron bed was a white cover which Mma had neatly embroidered.

It must be strange sleeping all on your own, thought Tiro. At home they all shared a room.

When the children noticed the electric light, Mma said they could try it. But after Tiro had flicked it on and off about ten times, Mma told him to stop.

Bringing the children close to her now, Mma sat down at last and asked them to tell her fully what had happened.

The Madam had made it clear to Mma that the police wouldn't like it if the children spent the night in Parktown. So when Naledi spoke about Grace and her offer to take them to Soweto, Mma seemed in two minds. She knew Grace's mother well, but Soweto was also dangerous.

After getting the Madam's permission to go out for a little, Mma took her children by the hand and they walked to number 17 in the next road. They went round to the back of the house and found Grace still there.

"These two will be just fine with me," Grace assured Mma.

It was arranged that Grace and the children would meet Mma at Johannesburg station at seven the next morning. Mma gave Grace some money for the fares and, close to tears again, she hugged the children goodbye.

"Cheer up, you two," said Grace. "You can come and meet my brothers."

Chapter Eight

POLICE

IT WAS RUSH-HOUR when they got on the train to Soweto and the children clung on tightly to Grace. There was no sitting space and it felt as if all their breath was being squeezed out of them. Grown-up bodies pressed in from above and all around them. Some people laughed, some people swore and others kept silent, as the train shook and lurched on its way.

At each station the crowd heaved towards the carriage door, people urgently pushing their way through. Naledi and Tiro tried to press backwards to stay close to Grace.

But in a sudden surge at one of the stations, they found themselves being carried forward, hurling out onto the platform. Desperately they tried to reach back to the open door, but passengers were still coming out, although the train was already beginning to move on.

Naledi was just able to see Grace wedged inside. She was trying to get out, but the train was on its way! Naledi and Tiro looked at each other in dismay. What now?

Everyone was walking towards the stairs which led to a bridge over the railway line. Soon the platform would be empty and the guard would see them. No tickets, no money, no idea of how they could find Grace. They would have to wait until she came back to get them, yet there was nowhere to hide on the platform.

"Let's go and look from the bridge," Naledi suggested.

Suddenly, without any warning, there was a commotion up ahead. Three figures in uniform stood at the top of the stairs.

Police!

People began turning around and coming rapidly back down. Some began running along the platform towards a high barbed-wire fence at the other end. The runners leapt at the fence and scrambled over it.

Others jumped down to the track, sprinted over the railway lines and clambered up to the opposite platform.

But just as they got there, more policemen appeared on that side.

"Where can we go?" Tiro urgently tugged at his sister's hand.

"We'll have to slip past them," she whispered, pulling him towards the stairs.

Some people were feeling into pockets, others frantically searching through bags.

Pass raid!

A man was protesting loudly that he had left his pass at home. It would only take two minutes to get it. The police could come and see, or someone could call his child to bring it. He cried out his address, once, twice...

Slap!

"*Hou jou bek*,"[1] barked the white officer in charge. His blue eyes stared coldly as a black policeman pushed the man against the wall.

One at a time people were pulled forward to be checked. When a boy said that he wasn't yet sixteen, the policeman just yelled he was a "liar" and a "loafer". Tiro felt his heart freeze, but the boy didn't cry. Instead his eyes seemed to have fire in them as he was handcuffed.

A voice in the crowd shouted, "Shame! Locking up children!"

[1] "shut up"

As the muttering grew louder, a woman spotted Naledi and Tiro and screamed, "You'll say these kids are sixteen next!"

The white officer took a threatening step forward. He looked murderous. Then, glancing at the children, he made a sign with his hand for them to go through.

"We can't stay on the bridge while the police are here," panted Naledi when they had got past. From the bridge they could see the road outside the railway station. Next to a large van were more police. An old woman was being pushed inside the van. Tiro looked back at the people in handcuffs on the bridge.

"Why don't we run and call the child to bring his father's pass? We heard the address so we can find it."

"Let's hurry then!" agreed Naledi.

Once past the police van, they asked a lady selling apples at the roadside to point out the way. The children weaved in and out of people as they ran along the stony road, between rows of grey block houses all looking exactly alike. No great leafy trees here, only grey smoke settling everywhere.

When they reached the right house, they found a boy struggling with a heavy tub. As soon as he understood their message, he dashed into the house, and a minute later came rushing out with a book in his hand.

All three raced back down the road, but just as they came in sight of the station, there was the big police van pulling off.

The boy shouted at it as it sped past them, carrying away his father. He flung the pass down, picked up a stone and let it fly at the van. The van swung round the corner, the stone just grazing the mudguard.

"I'll burn this one day!" stormed the boy, picking up his father's pass. "How can our parents put up with it?" There was fury in his voice. Then it became gentler. "Thanks anyway for trying… I must go and tell my mother now."

The children stood silently watching as he walked back home.

"Naledi! Tiro!"

Startled they looked around to find from where the voice was coming. It sounded quite far off.

Looking up towards the railway bridge, they saw Grace waving. Quickly they ran back to the station.

Grace came down with their tickets to get them through. It was a relief to be with her again.

"This time I'm really going to hold on to you," she told them, taking each firmly by the hand.

"Do you know what happened to us, Mma?" Tiro was anxious to tell Grace all.

Chapter Nine

THE PHOTOGRAPH

WHEN AT LAST they arrived at Grace's house, two boys, a little younger than Tiro, came racing out, then stopped short to look at Naledi and Tiro.

"Paul, Jonas. I've brought some friends for you," Grace announced.

Her brothers smiled shyly.

Inside the house was dark until Grace lit a lamp. The small room was almost filled by a table, a cupboard and stove.

"Hungry?" asked Grace. Four heads nodded.

It wasn't long before a good smell of beans was coming from the pot. Jonas and Paul brought out some wire cars and the younger children were soon busy discussing different things they had made, while Grace chatted with Naledi.

Before the meal, hands had to be washed at the tap outside the back door.

"Our people wash and clean up for others all day, but look how we must wash ourselves!" Grace spoke sharply.

Naledi wanted to ask Grace what she meant, but Tiro had begun splashing water.

"Stop it, Tiro! You're wasting water." Naledi made him come away from the tap. She explained how they had to buy water from the village tap at home.

"We used to get our water from the river, but it's all dried up now."

"Was your river very big?"

"Were there crocodiles?" Paul and Jonas, who had never been beyond Johannesburg, were curious!

It was while they were eating that Naledi noticed a small photograph on the wall of Grace's mother with four children. It had been taken some years ago, when Paul and Jonas were no more than babies.

"Who's this?" Naledi enquired, pointing to a boy who looked a few years older than Grace.

"That's our eldest brother, Dumi, but he isn't here

any more," replied Grace rather quietly.

"Where is he?" asked Tiro.

"If I tell you, you mustn't go shouting about it."

Naledi and Tiro shook their heads.

"But remember what Mma said, Grace. We mustn't talk about it, or Dumi will be in trouble." Paul looked very worried.

"It's all right," assured his older sister. "These two aren't big mouths like some kids round here."

By now Tiro and Naledi were looking quite puzzled.

"You see," Grace began, "our brother Dumi got picked up by the police, in '76. That was the time when the students here and all over were marching, and the place was on fire…"

Grace paused.

"You must know about it. Or were you too young then?"

"The older students at school sometimes talk about such things, but we don't know much," Naledi admitted.

So, with the dim light from the lamp flickering their shadows on the walls of the small room, Grace began to tell the children her story.

Chapter Ten

GRACE'S STORY

IT WAS A "time of fire" as Grace called it, when she and Dumi had marched in the streets with thousands of other schoolchildren. They were protesting that their schools taught them only what the white government wanted them to know.

On the banner that Dumi and his friends carried, they had written:

"BLACKS ARE NOT DUSTBINS."

Everything went all right until the police saw the schoolchildren marching, and then the trouble started. The police aimed their guns and began to shoot with real bullets, killing whoever was in the way.

It was terrible. The police shot tear gas too, making

everyone's eyes burn.

People were screaming, bleeding, falling. More police came in great steel tanks, and more in helicopters, firing from above. A little girl standing near Grace, about eight years old, raised her fist, and next thing she was lying dead.

People became fighting mad, throwing stones at the police, burning down schools and government offices. Smoke and flames were everywhere.

But the police kept shooting, until hundreds were dead. Hundreds were hurt and hundreds were arrested.

Dumi was one of those arrested.

When he came out of prison, he said that the police had beaten him up badly, but he would go on fighting even if they killed him.

Then one night he disappeared. When their mother went to each police station, asking if he was there, the police said "No". But maybe they were lying. Maybe they had killed him too. For a year they had no news.

Until one day a letter came. It was from Dumi. There was no address, but it had been posted in Johannesburg. Dumi wrote that he was well and studying in another country. He was giving the letter to a friend to post. He also wrote that he would be coming back one day. Coming back to help fight for FREEDOM and make life better for everyone. He had written FREEDOM in big letters.

The family had been so excited that he was alive, so worried about the dangers he faced, yet so proud of his courage. Dumi had been a boy when he left, but now he would be a man. Although it was a long time since they had heard from him, they hadn't given up hope. They were still waiting.

When Grace finished talking, the children remained quite silent.

"Well, it's time to sleep," Grace said, pushing back her chair and stretching herself up. Her young brothers cleared up the dishes, stacking them up ready to wash them outside in the morning.

Grace shared her bed with Naledi and the boys shared theirs with Tiro. He was soon fast asleep but Naledi lay awake for a while, thinking.

So much had happened. She wondered what her mother was doing. Was Mma alone in the little room in the yard, or was she still watching over the child in the big house?

Naledi was sure Mma must be thinking of Dineo. Why couldn't Mma have left straight away, and what if something happened to Dineo before they arrived? Naledi didn't want to think about that. At least the delay had led to them being with Grace, and she really liked Grace.

Her mind wandered over the terrible events in Soweto, to Dumi and to the word in big letters — FREEDOM. What did the word really mean? Did it mean they could live with their mother? Did it mean they could go to secondary school? But Grace said the children marched because they had to learn a lot of "rubbish" in school. So what would you learn in a school with FREEDOM?

There were so many questions, Naledi thought, as she drifted into sleep.

Chapter Eleven

JOURNEY HOME

"WAKE UP! IT'S five o'clock."

When Grace's voice reached Naledi and Tiro, they pulled themselves up. Silently they drank the tea Grace had made before slipping quietly out of the house, leaving Jonas and Paul still asleep.

It was half dark, but already many people were hurrying towards the station, and the train was crowded all over again. Most of the faces still looked tired. Bones squeezed against bones as they jolted, jerked and swayed with each movement of the train. At each station yet more bodies crammed in against them, until at last they were thrown out with the crowd rushing off to another day's work in Johannesburg.

When they arrived at the main ticket office, Mma was already waiting with her case. She thanked Grace warmly.

"Any time you need help, let me know," Mma added.

"*Tsamaya sentle*," Grace called as they parted at the barrier.

"*Sala sentle!*" They waved goodbye as they went.

The train going home wasn't crowded so the children sat by the window, hoping to see places they had passed on the way, especially the orange farm where they had spent the night. They told Mma about the boy who had helped them. She said quietly, "That was brave of him. He could have got into a lot of trouble."

"Mma, do you know Grace has a br—"

Tiro was beginning to talk about Dumi, but Naledi quickly nudged him with her foot and gave him a stern look. The scatterbrain! Already he was forgetting the promise they had made Grace. Tiro bit his lip, but fortunately Mma hadn't noticed anything.

"Those children should be in school," Mma continued, still thinking about the boy on the farm.

Naledi lay with her head against her mother's shoulder. It was so confusing. Here was Mma saying that children should be in school, and there was Grace saying that schools taught black children rubbish.

Didn't Dumi and his friends carry a poster saying "BLACKS ARE NOT DUSTBINS"?

What did Mma think about that and all the shooting? Had she heard about the little girl who was killed close to Grace? Mma had never spoken to them about such things. Did she think they were too young to be told?

Naledi stared out of the window, without seeing anything. Her mind was too full of questions. Surely she could talk to Mma about what was troubling her? As she leant against Mma's body and felt its warmth, it seemed silly to hold back problems. Especially when their time together was so short.

"Mma..." Naledi began, turning to look up at her mother's face. "Grace told us how the schoolchildren marched in the streets..."

Naledi stopped, seeing shock and pain flash through Mma's eyes. She became even more alarmed when Mma remained quite silent for what seemed like an age, gazing down at her lap.

At last, Mma spoke very softly. "Do you know how many children died on those streets? Do you know how many mothers were crying 'Where's my child'?"

Mma was shaking her head slowly. There was another

long pause, as if she was thinking whether to say any more. Then she leant forward and covered her face with one hand, wiping her forehead.

"You know, every day I must struggle… struggle… to make everything just how the Madam wants it. The cooking, the cleaning, the washing, the ironing. From seven every morning, sometimes till ten, even eleven at night, when they have their parties. The only time I sit is when I eat! But I keep quiet and do everything, because if I lose my job I won't get another one. This Madam will say I am no good. Then there will be no food for you, no clothes for you, no school for you."

Mma pulled her back up straight and put an arm around her children. Tiro shifted to come closer.

"It's very bad, Mma," Naledi said, in a low voice.

"Yes, it's bad. But those children who marched in the streets don't want to be like us… learning in school just how to be servants. They want to change what is wrong… even if they must die!"

"Oh, Mma, oh, Mma," Naledi whispered.

Tiro clutched Mma's hand and she pulled him towards her lap.

"What did their parents say?" he asked.

"Some tried to stop their children so they wouldn't

get hurt, but there were also parents who helped them."

Mma explained how the children had asked their parents not to work on certain days, and how many people had stayed at home. It had been a time of terrible worry for Mma's friends who had families in Soweto. The eldest Mbatha boy had been arrested and Mma told them about his mother's dreadful search at all the police stations.

So… Mma knew something about Dumi, Naledi thought. But neither she nor Tiro broke their own promise.

When Mma finished speaking, they sat in silence. They watched the train stop at stations on the way, passengers climbing in and out with cases, bags and bundles.

Vast stretches of land flashed by; grassland, mountains, grassland again. Naledi suddenly felt very small. Before this journey to fetch Mma, she had never imagined that all this land existed. Nor had she any idea of what the city was like. She had never known a person like Grace before, and she had never known her own mother in the way she was beginning to know her now…

★ ★ ★

"That's it. I'm sure that's it!"

Tiro's voice startled Naledi from her thoughts, but already the orange farm to which he was pointing was in the distance. Mma nodded with a slight smile.

Chapter Twelve

THE HOSPITAL

NONE OF THEM spoke after that, their thoughts all turned to Dineo. When the train pulled in at their station, Mma hurried the children out onto the platform. Outside, she spoke anxiously to a man standing against a car. After she had taken some notes from her purse, he agreed to take them first to their village and then go on to the hospital. So much money, thought Naledi. Mma must have borrowed it.

As the car bumped along the road into the village, churning up the dust, it seemed longer than two days that they had set off walking. Mma directed the driver to the house and people looked up as the car passed by. It wasn't often a car came this way. The sound of the engine brought Nono and Mmangwane outside. Nono looked so thin and weary, but her eyes lit up when she saw whom it was.

"The child is very sick," she whispered, in a low voice.

Mma rushed in and came out clasping Dineo close to her, the little girl lying limply in Mma's arms, her eyes sunken.

"You children must stay with Nono," Mma said firmly, as they struggled to bring the case out of the car.

"Oh, please, Mma, can't I come with you? Please?" Naledi pleaded. "Tiro can help Nono."

Mma looked across at Nono, whose tired face nodded "yes". Naledi gave her grandmother a quick hug.

"Thank you, Nono! Tiro will tell you everything… and please don't be angry with us. We're very sorry we gave you more worry."

"But we had to get Mma!" put in Tiro.

"Well, come in and tell us about it," invited Mmangwane.

Nono put an arm round Tiro's shoulders as they waved goodbye. From inside the car Naledi watched the little group grow smaller until they had quite disappeared behind the clouds of dust.

As the car now jerked its way back to the town over the rough roads, Mma cradled Dineo in her arms, whispering soft words to her. Naledi held Dineo's little hand, stroking and playing gently with her fingers. But the little girl made no response. Each minute on the way to the hospital now seemed important. What if they got there just a minute too late? That couldn't happen... could it?

At last they were travelling through the town, and then out into the open again, until there at last was a cluster of low white buildings with a few trees and bushes scattered between them. Some people were waiting by the roadside outside the hospital, and as soon as Mma and Naledi climbed out of the car, an old man came hobbling over to the driver. He was followed by others and almost immediately the car, packed tight with people, was rumbling off back to the town.

Naledi stayed close to Mma as she made her way past people sitting or lying down on the ground in front of the buildings. A lady with a thin blanket wrapped over her shoulders pointed the way.

Around the corner they found the queue of patients. It led up to a verandah where a woman in white sat at a desk.

"Is that the doctor for Dineo?" Naledi whispered.

Mma shook her head. "No. We must get a card first. The doctor is inside."

The queue moved very slowly as people shuffled forward after every few minutes. Some patients, who were too weak to stand, lay wedged against the wall and had to be helped along. Just in front of Mma and Naledi was a young woman with a small baby tied in a blanket to her back. Naledi wondered if the woman or the baby was the patient.

The sun shone down on the queue. Mma tried to screen Dineo from the glare, but the heat seemed to soak in everywhere and Dineo began to whimper. Mma tried rocking her gently, while Naledi tried singing her little songs which had always made her laugh. However, now Dineo didn't even seem to hear them...

When finally it was Mma's turn at the desk, Naledi relaxed a little. Now Dineo could go inside and be given medicine. But when Mma led the way down a corridor and into a room filled with far more people than had been outside, Naledi felt panic grip her.

"Are all these people before Dineo, Mma?" she cried, softly.

"They are also very sick, Naledi. We must be patient."

They were lucky to find space on a bench next to the young woman with the baby. She didn't look much older than Grace, thought Naledi.

It was the young woman who spoke first.

"It's always long to wait. I was here before with my baby and now he's sick again."

"What's the problem?" Mma asked.

"Last time the doctor said he must have more milk,

but I've no money to buy it."

Mma sighed. "I think it's the same sickness with my child."

Chapter Thirteen

LIFE AND DEATH

ALL THROUGH THE afternoon, they watched the patients being called one at a time by the nurse. Once the doctor himself came out. His face seemed nearly as white as his coat, except for the dark shadows under his eyes.

By mid-afternoon, Dineo needed water, but when Mma carried her to a small fountain in one corner, she almost turned away. It was so dirty! Naledi came over and struggled to cup some water in her hand without touching the sides. Then she let the water dribble over Dineo's dry little lips.

Naledi now began to feel her own empty stomach twist and turn. Her last meal had been with Grace the night before. Mma seemed to read her thoughts and sent her out to see what she could buy for a few cents. When Naledi came back with three small buns, Mma offered one to the young woman. From the way she ate it, Naledi could tell that she was very hungry too.

It was only after the light had begun to fade outside that the young woman was called to take her baby to the doctor. The child had been very quiet all afternoon, wrapped snugly against its mother's back.

In a very little time the young woman came out of the doctor's room, clutching a plastic bag. Her whole body was shaking and a man close to the door caught her just as her legs gave way.

"My baby, my baby... he's dead, he's dead!"

Her sobs filled the waiting room. Before Mma could go to comfort her, the nurse reappeared calling for Dineo. The sobbing pierced Naledi's mind. She heard Mma telling her to stay where she was and she watched numbly as her little sister was now carried away. Then Naledi's gaze shifted to the plastic bag. The little baby had seemed to be sleeping so peacefully just a few minutes ago. Was it already dead then?

With head bowed, almost buried in the parcel, the young woman forced herself up and stumbled out of the waiting room. Naledi's eyes now fixed on the doctor's door, but instead she saw a plastic parcel being laid in a grave. It made her want to run to Mma. She sat gripping tightly onto her seat.

When Mma finally returned, her arms were empty.

"What happened, Mma?" Naledi cried.

"We must leave Dineo here and I must come back in three days... her throat is very bad... and her body is too weak..." Mma's voice sounded choked.

Before leaving Mma had to pay at the desk. There would be more to pay later, so she checked the remaining notes in her purse.

"We've nothing for bus fare... we'll just have to walk home."

Mma looked drained.

"But it's not so far as Jo'burg, Mma!" Naledi put her arm through Mma's. She was surprised at her own sudden confidence when only a little while ago she had wanted to run to Mma for comfort herself. Well, at least they had each other.

Outside it was dark, but the moon fortunately lit the road and Mma knew a way which avoided the town. So with arms linked, they set off on the long walk home.

On the way Naledi asked about the doctor. Mma said

they were lucky because he had been very gentle with Dineo, although he looked sick himself from tiredness.

"Did he say Dineo will get better, Mma?"

"We can only hope, my child…" Mma paused and pressed Naledi's hand. "I'm thankful you came for me. We must hope the medicine will save her."

The doctor had also told Mma that Dineo needed milk, fruit and vegetables to keep her body strong.

"But he didn't tell me how to find the money to buy them all," Mma added quietly.

By the time they reached their village, the moon had moved far across the dark sky. Nono stirred as they entered the house. She had been waiting anxiously for their return. Naledi could hardly keep her eyes open while she drank the tea Nono gave her. She crept under the blanket, finishing her last mouthful.

Chapter Fourteen

WAITING

IT WAS USUALLY a good time for the children when Mma was at home. First there would be the excitement of waiting for her to arrive and then the flurry of greetings, hugs and news. Later, Mma would open her case and bring out the presents she had been saving for the family. On her 'day off' in the city, she sometimes went to jumble sales to buy the clothes white people no longer wanted. Then would follow the pleasure of days when Mma would be around the house – helping Nono with the work, or playing with Dineo, and always ready to listen to the children's stories about what they had been doing.

But this time was different – like the time when Mma came just after Rra died.

The three days of waiting before Mma had to return to the hospital passed slowly. The grown-ups didn't speak of their worst fear, although Naledi saw the heavy, worried look in their eyes. Each morning Tiro asked Mma how much longer it was until she had to collect Dineo. Then, after he had helped bring the water, he would go off to play for short periods, but Naledi preferred to stay all the while at home with Mma.

On the fourth day Mma set off very early, alone. She had borrowed just enough money from a neighbour to pay for her bus fare to and from the hospital. That day seemed to pass even more slowly. Tiro stayed right outside the house fiddling with a piece of wire, changing its shape many times, then using it to draw in the sand. When Naledi wasn't busy, she came and sat on the doorstep, gazing out at the road. She forced her mind to stay blank, just searching the distance for any figures coming from the direction of the big road, where the bus would stop. She didn't want to think about what was happening in the hospital, because it would bring back the picture of the plastic bag.

From time to time, Naledi would see the vague shape of a woman appear with a baby wrapped to her back, but as she came closer, Naledi would see it wasn't Mma. It was late in the afternoon when at last there was a figure which really did seem to be Mma. Naledi called out to Nono, who was in the house, and she and Tiro began racing up the dusty road.

"It's Mma! It is!" Tiro shouted as they ran.

"Dineo's on her back!" Naledi panted.

As the two children came sprinting towards her, Mma stopped and turned a little so they could see their sister. As the children greeted her, she gave a shy smile, resting her head on Mma's shoulder.

"She's still quite weak, but her fever has gone," said Mma.

With Naledi and Tiro either side of her, Mma walked on to the house. Mmangwane came up the road, calling out in delight. Nono remained at the door, holding on to the side for support.

"My child," she whispered, as she put out her hand to touch Dineo's head.

Chapter Fifteen

HOPE

THAT NIGHT THE children found it hard to get to sleep. Mma had to return to the city the next morning as each day she was losing pay.

There was all the borrowed money to pay back now, as well as the money to send Nono each month for food, school and all the other expenses. Mma was clearly worried about Dineo not getting enough milk. The nurse had repeated what the doctor had told Mma about Dineo needing milk, fruit and vegetables.

"But we work very hard and earn very little," Mma had said with a sigh as she cuddled Dineo, before putting her down to sleep.

Tiro had said goodnight, but lay thinking about the boy on the orange farm. He wondered if he himself was old enough to go and find work. But he knew Mma wouldn't agree. Hadn't she said the children working on the farm should be in school?

Then he thought of Dumi and the bit in the letter about studying in another country. Studying what? Tiro wondered. He would ask Naledi tomorrow…

Tomorrow he would also remake his wire car and try out Jonas and Paul's design. Putting out his arm, he touched Dineo. It was lovely knowing she was there again. If only Mma didn't have to go away now…

Naledi lay awake too, listening to the murmuring voices of Nono, Mmangwane and Mma. It was so comforting to hear them all together. But tomorrow night Mma's voice would be missing.

Naledi buried her head in her arms, forcing back her tears. Crying wouldn't help. She couldn't imagine Grace crying and Grace had to look after her young brothers and the house all by herself most of the time. Yet Grace had said things in a way that made you feel better, like when she had said, "We're pushed all over the place, but it won't be like that for ever."

But when would they see Grace again? It occurred to Naledi that at least they could write to each other. Tomorrow she must ask Mma to find out Grace's address.

Then a new idea came to her. Wasn't it possible that in her own school there were people like Grace? Naledi had overheard bits of conversations amongst the older students, although she had never taken much notice before. But why shouldn't she begin to talk to them and become friends, even if she was a little younger? If they heard she had been to Johannesburg, they would be interested, she was sure.

What was it Mma had said about the children in Soweto? That they didn't want to learn just to be servants. Oh yes, they were right.

All of a sudden, lying there in the dark, it became so clear to Naledi. It wasn't just *their* schools they were talking about. It was *her* school too. All those lessons on writing letters… for jobs as servants… always writing how good they were at cooking, cleaning, washing, gardening… always ending with "Yours obediently".

Naledi had never thought about it before tonight, but never, never, had she written about wanting to be… say, a doctor. Yes, that's what she'd like to be. Imagine how useful it would be if she became a doctor. Especially in their own village, she could even look after her own family.

For a few moments, Naledi lay imagining herself in a long white coat, in a bright room with shining

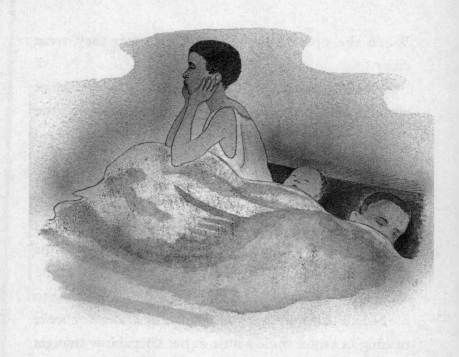

cupboards all around her (like the cupboards where Mma worked). Then something jarred...

She saw in her mind someone bringing her a little baby. The mother looked like the young woman in the queue at the hospital and the baby was so thin that its little rib bones pushed up from under its skin. The mother was clearly poor and had no food for her child.

Where would she, the doctor, get food for the baby?

When she opened her shining cupboards they were empty.

Naledi then began to imagine a whole line of mothers and grandmothers bringing weak, thin little babies up to her. What could she do?

For a while she felt the tears pressing on her eyelids again. No! She wouldn't give in to tears. It was just that she couldn't work this all out by herself. Well, school would be starting again in a week. That wasn't long. At break time she would go where the older students usually sat chatting. Just wait till they heard where she and Tiro had been.

Naledi turned over and stroked Dineo's cheek, making her sister smile a little in her sleep. How strange, thought Naledi. If Dineo hadn't been so terribly ill, she and Tiro would never have made the journey to get Mma. It had saved Dineo, she was sure. But also through this journey, she had begun to find out so much…

The grown-up voices had stopped and Naledi heard Mma blow out the lamp and quietly shift into bed. Naledi's eyelids were heavy and she felt sleep pulling at her. She fell asleep at last, picturing her first day back at school, surrounded by friends, old and new.

Postscript

Journey to Jo'burg was a journey for me as well as for Naledi and Tiro. You see, when I was growing up, I was the child who had two mothers. I had my own mother as well as a different mother who, although she was looking after me, really belonged to some other children. I knew her as "Mary", but her proper name was Mma Sebate. The laws of South Africa at that time even forbade her own children to live with her — because her family was black. Ours was white. Those terrible laws had been made by the whites-only government and were part of what was called apartheid (which in English means "separation").

I was born and brought up in Johannesburg, "Jo'burg" for short. We did not live in a great big pink house like the Madam in this book, but in a small flat. My strongest memory of my mother is of her tapping away at her typewriter. She wrote about the theatre and made radio programmes, and my dad was a music publisher who wrote musicals. We were all looked after by Mary, who was cook, cleaner and nanny. As a child I never questioned the fact that I called her by her first name when all white adults had to be called Aunty, Uncle, Mr or Mrs. I never questioned that we called her by an English name when her first language was Tswana. I never questioned that her own children lived 150 miles away and that she only saw them when our family went on holiday. One awful day, when I was about eleven, she received a telegram and collapsed in front of me. The telegram told her that two of her three young daughters (aged about three and five at the time) had died. They had had diphtheria – a disease that I, as a white child, could not have caught. I had been vaccinated. Her children had not.

It was only years later that I began to ask questions about the way we lived and everything that, as a child, I had simply accepted. This was after I had left my whites-only school and was at university. The government had passed a law to stop black students studying with white students, but fortunately there were still a few black students at the university. And when Nelson Mandela and his comrades were arrested, both black and white students protested together. My brother was busy with secret anti-apartheid activity and I also got involved. In 1964 we were both arrested. I was let out after eight weeks but my brother was put on trial and sentenced to two years in jail.

Of course, for black South Africans the whole country was like a vast jail. If Naledi and Tiro's mother in *Journey to Jo'burg* had lost her job, she could have lost her "permission" to stay in Jo'burg. She could then have been arrested and thrown into jail simply because her "pass" was not in order.

I have often wondered how, as a child, I never really saw or understood how shocking apartheid and racism were. Our mother was Jewish and I had wept over *The Diary of Anne Frank*. If we had lived in Europe, I knew that *I* could have been like Anne Frank. Why had I not seen the terrible things happening around me? When I began to remove my blinkers I felt angry. None of the teachers at my church school had asked me to THINK. I was also angry that I had only been allowed to choose my friends amongst people of the same skin colour. It was as stupid as saying you could only have friends of the same eye colour.

Years later, in England, with children of my own, I wanted to find a way of telling them about South Africa. Their father's grandparents had come from India to South Africa; now, apartheid laws forbade us to live together in our home country. I wanted my children, as well as others in England and elsewhere, to ask questions. By this time many black South African children were refusing to go to schools which they said only taught them to be servants, and the government was sending police and soldiers to arrest or shoot them. Yet in England, even in non-fiction books, young people were still not being told what was really happening in South Africa.

Postscript

I have always loved stories, and had begun to think about a story I especially wanted to tell, about two children whose baby sister falls desperately ill while their mother is working far away in Jo'burg. I wanted to show their courage in making the journey to save baby Dineo (which means "Special Gift" in Tswana). Because it is their first visit to the city, much of what they see is new to them. I hoped that my readers would join Naledi ("Morning Star") and Tiro ("Hard Work") in beginning to ask lots of questions about the way things were.

As the idea for my story grew, I was lucky to meet a South African called Ethel de Keyser. She worked for the British Defence and Aid Fund for Southern Africa, which helped families of people like Nelson Mandela who were in jail because of the fight for equality. Ethel and a few volunteers were encouraging children in Britain to find out more about apartheid. When I needed a publisher for my story, it was Ethel who kept me going when the first few publishers said "No thank you". *Journey to Jo'burg* was my first story and if I had been on my own, I might have given up and packed it away in a drawer. But with the support of Ethel and the group, the search went on until a "Yes" letter came!

I sent two copies of the first edition of the book to

nephews and nieces in South Africa. But my sister-in-law never got the parcel. Instead she received a letter headed UNDESIRABLE PUBLICATION: *A Journey to Jo'burg* – 2 COPIES. The books had been seized and banned by the government! They were only taken off the banned list the year after Nelson Mandela was let out of jail.

Now the government is chosen by *all* South African people, black and white, and there are no more apartheid laws. But Naledi and Tiro's story still carries many echoes.

BEVERLEY NAIDOO

COLLINS MODERN CLASSICS

✧

The Phantom Tolbooth

by

Norton Juster

"It seems to me that almost everything is a waste of time," Milo remarks glumly. But his glumness soon turns to surprise when he finds in his bedroom an enormous package marked: "One Genuine Turnpike Tollbooth". Milo points his little car towards the strange land that lies beyond the Phantom Tollbooth – the Kingdom of Wisdom. But it is a world full of extraordinary and unexpected hazards...

Collins *Children's Books*

Visit the book lover's website
www.fireandwater.com

COLLINS MODERN CLASSICS

✜

When Hitler Stole Pink Rabbit

by

Judith Kerr

Anna is too busy with school work and tobogganing to listen to the grown-ups' talk of Hitler. But one day she and her brother are rushed out of Germany in alarming secrecy. Their father is wanted by the Nazis – dead or alive. It is the start of a huge adventure; sometimes frightening, often funny, and always, always exciting…

Collins*Children'sBooks*

Visit the book lover's website
www.fireandwater.com